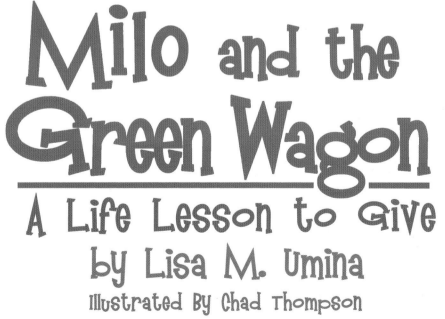

Milo and the Green Wagon
A Life Lesson to Give
by Lisa M. Umina
Illustrated By Chad Thompson

Milo and the Green Wagon
Text Copyright © 2008 Lisa M. Umina
Illustrations Copyright © 2008 by Lisa M. Umina

Editor Diana Donlon
Cover Design by Chad Thompson
Printed in China

Library of Congress Control Number: 2007941247
ISBN 13: 978-0-9797429-4-1
ISBN 10: 0-9797429-4-3

Published by

Halo
Publishing International®

6415 Granger Road, Independence, Ohio 44131
www.halopublishing.com

Author School Programs visit:
www.shoutlife.com/miloandlisa

Solutions to Hunger visit:
www.ACTMission.org

This book is dedicated to Rafaela, my muse. I am inspired by the loving heart you have and the driving passion you live by. You are my rock and my shield.

A special thank you goes out to all behind the scenes: my mother Victoria, my brothers David, Nick, Sonny, and sister-in-law Lisa, my stepbrother Michael, my stepparents Patrick and Phyllis, my grandmothers Angie and Regina, my nephews David and Kyle, and my Godchild Megan. You are my life, my love and the words I live by.

Additional thanks to: The Cruz Hernandez family, and my friends who are my family.

The spirit of this book is in memory of my father and my music man, John Umina and Señor Abel Cruz

Ultimate thanks to God who makes all things possible in my life.

Milo woke up one morning, stretched his arms and said, "God, today I want to make a difference!"

As he walked down the street to visit his friend Mary, he noticed an old, beat-up wagon in the garbage. Milo wondered, "Why would someone want to throw away a wagon?"

"The wagon has all of its wheels, but it needs to be painted," he thought. "I'll take it with me to show my friends."

Milo rescued the wagon and continued on his way to Mary's house.

When Milo arrived, Mary asked, "Milo, what are you doing with that ugly, green wagon?"

"I found it in the garbage while I was walking to your house," Milo replied. "I have a great idea about how we can use it. First, let's go to Matt's house."

Off they went.

"Hi, Milo and Mary," said Matt. "What are you doing with that ugly, green wagon? Where did you even find that thing?"

"Milo found it in the garbage," said Mary. "He has a great idea that he wants to share with us!"

"What's your idea, Milo?" asked Mark. "What are we going to do with the wagon?"

"I want us to help people," said Milo. "When I left church last Sunday, I noticed that people had donated food through the church's food drive. That got me thinking of how many people are faced with difficult situations."

Everyone looked at each other and then at the green wagon. The boys and Mary ran into the garage with the wagon.

"What color do you want to paint the wagon?" asked Mary.

"Let's keep it green," said Mark.

As the children began to paint the old wagon, they realized that their mission was missing a name. They thought of many names – the 4M Mission, the ABC mission, but none seemed to fit.

"Well, what do you think about ACT Mission?" suggested Milo. "Action Changes Things!"

"That's perfect!" said Matt.

Mark also agreed.

"The wagon looks great!" said Matt. "But listen to this wheel. It still squeaks."

"That's okay. It still works," added Milo.

"Hey, Matt, here comes your mom! Let's show her the wagon!" said Mary.

"Mom, Milo found an old wagon and we fixed it up!" said Matt.

"Good job painting the wagon! What does ACT stand for?" asked Matt's mom.

"ACT means Action Changes Things. It's the name of our new mission!" replied Mark.

"Mom, can you walk with us around the neighborhood to help collect donations?" asked Matt.

"YES, I would love to help you," said Matt's mom.

Off they went …

They walked next door
to Mr. Baker's house.

"Mr. Baker would you like to help the
ACT Mission by donating food, school supplies, or clothes?" asked Mark.

"Yes, I'd be glad to help. I have some canned fruit and vegetables and blankets for
your mission," said Mr. Baker.

The next house they visited was the Cruz family. They donated children's books, toys, and baby food. When the ACT Mission group arrived at Mrs. Madison's house, she donated six bags of baby clothes.

"People have been so generous," Milo said.

It didn't take long for word to get out about the ACT Mission.

Mark's neighbor Betty had just finished grocery shopping when Milo asked, "Would you like to help the ACT Mission by donating food?"

Betty placed an entire bag of groceries into the ACT Mission wagon.

Milo noticed that Betty wiped a tear of joy from her eye after she made her donation.

Later that afternoon, Betty called the church in the neighborhood and told Father Pete that Milo and his friends formed the ACT Mission and spent the whole day collecting food and clothes.

When the ACT Mission arrived back at the garage, they saw Father Pete waiting for them in the driveway.

"Look, there's Father Pete!" said Matt.

"You won't believe what has happened today," added Mary.

Matt opened the garage door to show Father Pete what they had collected.

"Wow! Look at the bags of clothes, and all of the toys and food," Father Pete said.

"Can you believe this, Father Pete?" asked Milo. "Look at how generous our neighbors are. Isn't this amazing!?"

"Yes!" said Father Pete. "I can believe their generosity because you decided to do something special and you gave of yourselves all day. You all are heroes. Your neighbors were inspired by your passion, and I'm here because I am proud of the ACT Mission!"

"Father, will you help us take these donations to the church?" asked Milo.

"Yes! And tomorrow I am visiting the shelter homes, and I would like all of you to join me to deliver your donations," said Father Pete.

The next day, Father Pete and Matt's mom drove the ACT Mission to the shelter homes.

Milo was anxious to see what the families would do with the gifts. He watched as the children excitedly opened their bags of toys and clothes. Milo also watched a mother cover her feet with a pair of socks.

As the ACT Mission team walked back to their van, Mary noticed a man sleeping on a park bench.

"Do we have a blanket for the man sleeping on the park bench?" asked Mary.

Matt's mom replied, "Yes, here's a soft, blue blanket."

Mary gently covered the man and said, "This should keep you warm."

The man opened his eyes, smiled and said, "Thank you."

It took the entire day to give away everything they had collected.

Father Pete was so touched by this experience that he asked, "Would the ACT Mission team like to be a part of tomorrow's sermon and share this miracle with the entire congregation?"

Milo looked at his friends. They all shook their heads and exclaimed, "Yes!"

That night, Milo went to bed and thought about his incredible day. He began to talk to God.

"Hi God," said Milo. "Thank you for guiding me to the green wagon. I am amazed at how a little wagon and a simple idea turned into what Father Pete called a *miracle*. Amen."

The next morning, as Sunday service was about to begin, Father Pete noticed that the ACT Mission team was missing one member … Milo.

"Where is Milo?" Father Pete asked Mary. "We need him and the wagon."

"I don't know," said Mary.

"Well, I'm sorry, we will have to start without him," said Father Pete.

When it was time for the sermon, Father Pete said, "I would like to invite the ACT Mission team to the altar to share what I call, 'A Life Lesson to Give.'"

Mary took a moment, drew a deep breath, and slowly walked to the altar.

She adjusted the microphone and was just about to speak when she was interrupted by a curious noise from the back of the church. As she looked toward the church doors, she stared in amazement and said, "Look, there's Milo!"

The people cheered.

"Who's in the wagon?"

"Where did he come from?"

Milo pulled the wagon *toward the altar* as he smiled and listened to the people ask questions.

Father Pete noticed there was more than a blue blanket in the wagon.

"I am sorry I am late," said Milo, "but I wanted to bring someone special to service today. He wants to say thank you."

As Milo approached the altar the people stood silent. The man slowly climbed out of the ACT Mission wagon and walked up to the altar.

"He looks familiar, doesn't he?" said a woman in the front pew.

"Yes, look at his dark brown hair, thick beard, and blue eyes," whispered her daughter.

The man stood at the podium and began to speak.

"Thank you," he said. "It is in the little things you do that miracles are created, when we do for the least of our brothers, we do for God." *Matthew 25:40*

The man walked down the aisle and continued to smile as he walked out of the church.

Milo ran after him.

"Where is my new friend?" he thought. "I must know his name!"

When Milo stood outside, he realized he was too late. His friend was already gone.

Milo wondered, "Was my friend Jesus, or was he the stranger they saw on the park bench?"

His question was answered as he heard the people in the church sing, "What so ever you do to the least of my brothers, so you do onto me . . . . "

"That's it!" Milo thought as he walked back into the church, "Jesus Christ is inside all of us."

As the service continued, an overwhelming peace filled the hearts of each and every person.

As the people walked out of the church at the end of the service, Mary said, "Look at the cross in the garden!"

"Thank you God," whispered Milo.